UNVEILED

A FATHER'S REFLECTIONS ON LIFE

KOYIDALA SATISH

Made with ♥ on the Notion Press Platform
www.notionpress.com

Dedicated to my beloved Aunt Pragada Annapurna,
Who raised me as her own with boundless love,
Your nurturing embrace and unwavering care,
Shaped me into the person I am today.

Contents

Foreword

A Father's Legacy

In the realm of words and ink, where stories breathe life and emotions dance on the pages, I found myself captivated by a tale that pulses with the heartbeat of a father's love.

It is a narrative that transcends the boundaries of time and space, weaving a tapestry of profound connection between a father and his beloved son.

Within these pages, the profound bond between a father and his son comes alive—a story of love, guidance, and an enduring connection.

It is a tale that resonates with the timeless wisdom a father imparts, shaping his son's path through heartfelt moments.

Through this captivating narrative, we are reminded of the profound love that transcends time and the enduring values that shape our lives.

Dear reader, as you embark on this literary voyage, I invite you to surrender yourself to its embrace. Allow the words to wash over you, igniting the flickering flames of love and remembrance within your own heart.

May this story resonate deeply, reminding you of the profound influence of a father's love, and inspiring you to embrace the values that endure.

Preface

In the hallowed pages that lie before you, dear reader, a tale of love, loss, and the haunting embrace of destiny unfolds.

Welcome to the ethereal realm of my words, woven with strands of melancholy and whispered secrets.

It is a world where sorrow dances with longing, and where the echoes of forgotten memories reverberate through the very fabric of existence.

Within these chapters, you shall journey alongside souls burdened by the weight of their pasts, souls yearning to unearth the truths that lie hidden within the depths of their hearts.

Prepare to immerse yourself in a narrative that transcends the boundaries of time and space, for it is a story that binds together the threads of human experience and the enigmatic forces that shape our lives.

Like a mournful ballad that drifts on the wind, the tales of this book will transport you to the mist-shrouded streets of Ravenshade, a town haunted by both its tragic history and the ghosts that linger in its alleys.

Here, you will encounter characters whose souls bear the scars of unrequited love, shattered dreams, and the pursuit of redemption.

Through the lens of my words, you will witness the interplay of light and darkness, love and loss, hope and despair.

Prepare to traverse the intricate tapestry of emotions as you delve into the depths of human existence, guided by the hand of fate and the whispers of forgotten voices.

Each page holds a piece of a puzzle waiting to be solved, secrets yearning to be unveiled.

But be forewarned, dear reader, for the journey ahead is not one for the faint of heart. Within these chapters, you will confront the depths of sorrow and the fragility of hope.

Yet, amidst the melancholic melodies that permeate this world, you may discover the indomitable strength of the human spirit and the transformative power of love.

So, embrace the shadows that dance upon these pages and allow the melodies of longing to stir your soul. For in this realm of whispered tales and forgotten dreams, you will find a reflection of your own joys and sorrows, your own triumphs and tribulations.

May the words that follow ignite the embers of your imagination, and may you find solace in the bittersweet symphony of life's fleeting moments. Welcome, dear reader, to the poetic world of ravaged hearts and eternal whispers.

Let us embark together on this enigmatic journey and see where the paths of destiny lead us.

Yours in the shadows,

koyidala Satish.

Acknowledgements

I would like to express my heartfelt gratitude to my friend and brother, Raj Santosh, for his invaluable support and guidance.

I am deeply indebted to him for his unwavering friendship and constant encouragement throughout my journey.

His presence in my life has been a source of strength and inspiration. I am truly fortunate to have such a remarkable individual by my side, and I sincerely thank him for his unwavering belief in me.

INSPIRED FROM TRUE STORIES

Disclaimer

This work of fiction is a product of the author's imagination. Any resemblance to actual persons, living or deceased, or events is purely coincidental. The characters, places, and incidents portrayed in this book are entirely fictitious.

No Offense Intended: The purpose of this book is to entertain and captivate readers through storytelling. It does not seek to offend or harm any individual, group, or community. The author holds deep respect for diversity, and any similarities to real-world elements are coincidental.

Mahakavi Sri Sri's profound words resonate with wisdom and truth, emphasizing the remarkable depth and richness found within the pages of the Bhagavatam. In this timeless epic, Hindu mythology unfolds its intricate tapestry, weaving together tales of love, friendship, and the human experience.

It is a treasure trove of invaluable lessons and insights that can guide us on our journey through life.Inspired by the profound teachings of Hindu mythology, I embarked on a creative endeavor, pouring my heart and soul into the creation of this book

As I delved into the vast expanse of Hindu mythology, I discovered a treasure trove of wisdom that transcended the pages of ancient scriptures.

The stories and teachings echoed through the ages, carrying timeless messages of compassion, courage, and the eternal search for meaning. They offered glimpses into the human psyche, exploring the depths of our desires, aspirations, and the indomitable spirit that propels us forward.

In writing this book, I sought to honor the essence of Hindu mythology and its profound teachings. It is my humble attempt to pay homage to the wisdom passed down through generations, inviting readers to embark on a journey of self-reflection and discovery.

Within these pages, I hope to ignite the spark of curiosity, to inspire contemplation, and to evoke a sense of wonder about the vast and intricate tapestry of life.

As you delve into the chapters of this book, I invite you to immerse yourself in the magic and wisdom of Hindu mythology. Allow the ancient tales to illuminate your path, to offer solace in times of uncertainty, and to remind you of the timeless truths that resonate within us all.

May this journey through the realms of imagination and introspection awaken a renewed sense of wonder and a deeper understanding of the human experience.

CHAPTER ONE

Shadows Of Solitude

In the sorrowful town of Ravenshade, young kshayank life was colored by a haunting sense of loss. Once, his world had been filled with the radiant warmth of his father's love, but fate had cruelly snatched that joy away.

It was a tragic tale, one that echoed through the mist-laden streets, whispered by the wind in mournful tones.

kshayank's father, a figure of strength and wisdom, had been taken from him too soon. The details surrounding his untimely demise remained shrouded in ambiguity, leaving kshayank with unanswered questions that gnawed at his soul.

The void left by his father's absence permeated every aspect of his existence, casting a melancholic shadow over his tender heart.

The memories of his father lingered like ethereal whispers, haunting him day and night. A mere glimpse of a photograph, a forgotten trinket, or the scent of his father's favorite cologne would evoke a bittersweet symphony of emotions within Kshayank.

Tears would well in his eyes as he yearned for the presence he could no longer embrace, his heart aching with an insatiable longing.

In the quiet solitude of his room, kshayank would often retreat, surrounded by mementos and fragments of a shattered past. His father's absence loomed large, an invisible specter that weighed heavily upon his weary shoulders.

The laughter they once shared, the stories his father would tell, now resided in the realm of fading memories, their vibrant hues dulled by the passage of time.

CHAPTER TWO

Eternal Words

In the dimly lit attic of an old ancestral home, dust particles danced in the sun's feeble rays that filtered through the small, forgotten window. The air was heavy with the weight of forgotten memories and hidden secrets, as if the very walls whispered tales of bygone eras.

It was in this forgotten corner of time that young kshayank stumbled upon a worn leather-bound journal. As he carefully brushed off the layers of neglect, the initials "k.S." were revealed, embossed in faded gold letters on the cover.

A shiver ran down his spine as he realized it belonged to his late father, the enigmatic koyidala Satish.

My dear unborn son,

Within the abyss of remorse, I pen this letter, burdened by the weight of our collective sins. We, the architects of our own demise, have left you a ravaged world, a legacy of chaos and devastation.

It is with a heavy heart that I implore your forgiveness for the transgressions of our generation, for we have sowed the seeds of our own destruction.

Once, people planted trees, nurturing the Earth for future generations, but we, driven by insatiable greed, mercilessly felled them. We severed the lifelines that connected us to the very essence of existence, forsaking the wisdom of our forefathers. Now, the desolation surrounds us, and the barren landscape bears witness to our selfishness.

Once, people cherished the harmonious embrace of nature and animals, recognizing their inherent value. But we, in our arrogance, betrayed both, heedless of the intricate tapestry of life that we disrupted.

The consequences of our betrayal reverberate through the hollow chambers of our souls, as we realize too late the depth of our folly.

We created a world where the air hangs heavy with fear, where masks shield us from the invisible specter that haunts our every step.

Our shortsightedness and disregard for the delicate balance of nature have thrust us into a realm of uncertainty and isolation. The very air we breathe has become a reminder of our own vulnerability, a testament to our failure.

In our pursuit of progress, we neglected to teach the fundamental truth of equality. We failed to impart the knowledge that equality extends beyond gender, that it encompasses all living organisms that share this fragile planet. We transgressed against the very essence of our being, blind to the interconnectedness that binds us all.

I apologize deeply for the state of this world we have bequeathed you, ravaged by our insatiable greed. The destructive path we believed to be progress has left a trail of devastation in its wake. I hope, with all my heart, that you can find it in yourself to forgive us for the mess we have created.

Regrettably, we have not left you with the inheritance you deserve. Our misguided priorities and unquenchable desires have led us astray, neglecting the responsibility to leave behind a better world for future generations. We were blinded by the false allure of material wealth and failed to recognize the true treasures of this planet.

Once, I believed that the growth of cities and the façade of "civilization" would elevate humanity. But alas, we have proven to be no different than the wild creatures that roam the untouched forests. The violence embedded in our DNA continues to consume us, and it grieves me to witness how little we have truly evolved.

It is a bitter truth to accept, but one that we must face. Our betrayal of nature has led to our own betrayal, as the consequences of our actions unfold relentlessly.

we are still the same savage creatures, just wearing fancier clothes."

My son, I implore you to learn from our mistakes, to break the cycle of destruction, and to find a path that embraces harmony with the natural world.

May you transcend the limitations of our savage past and guide humanity towards a future where greed is replaced with compassion, where progress aligns with the well-being of both the planet and its inhabitants.

Please forgive us, my dear unborn son, for our failures as stewards of this Earth. I entrust you with the hope that you will rise above the darkness that has consumed us and bring forth a brighter tomorrow.

At the end of these pages, as I pour my heart out to you, my dear unborn son, there is one last story I wish to share—a tale of resilience, hope, and the power of redemption.

As I pen these final words, know that my spirit is intertwined with yours, urging you forward on this journey of healing and restoration. I may not be there physically, but my love and guidance will always be with you, embedded within the stories passed down through generations.

I beseech you, my beloved son, to find it in your heart to forgive us. Forgive us for the broken world we leave in our wake, for the shattered dreams and hopes that should have been yours.

May our remorse serve as a catalyst for change, igniting a fire within you to reclaim what has been lost and to forge a future built upon empathy, compassion, and reverence for all life.

With a sorrow that knows no bounds,

Your repentant father

.KOYIDALA SATISH.

CHAPTER THREE

Lost Echoes

Ruhi stood in a realm cloaked in uncertainty, a place where the boundaries of existence seemed hazy and the sense of self was elusive. Perplexed and lost, he yearned for answers—yearned to understand the nature of his being and the purpose of his presence in this enigmatic realm.

Ruhi's confusion lingered, his mind clouded with questions and a yearning for clarity. In the midst of his disarray, a strange voice, resounding with a sense of authority and compassion, broke through the veil of uncertainty.

"My dear son," the voice called out, resonating with a gentle power that seemed to originate from the very essence of creation, "come with me. I will take you to the peace you seek."

Ruhi's curiosity grew even stronger, and he yearned to understand what this "peace" truly entailed. With a cautious tone, he asked, "But what is this 'peace' you speak of? How can I trust that it is what I truly need?"

The voice, radiating warmth and understanding, responded, "Peace, my dear son, is a state of inner tranquility, a harmony that transcends the chaos of the world.

It is the serenity that comes from embracing your true self and aligning with your purpose. Trust that deep within you, there lies a yearning for this peace, a yearning to discover your place in the grand tapestry of existence."

My dear voice," Ruhi retorted with a hint of arrogance, his voice laced with a self-assured confidence, "you speak of peace as if it is some elusive prize I should blindly pursue. But let me make one thing clear—I am not one to easily trust in empty promises."

The voice, undisturbed by Ruhi's audacity, responded with unwavering calmness, "Ah, my dear son, you misunderstand my intentions. I offer you not empty promises, but the gateway to a realm where peace reigns supreme. It is a realm befitting one of such discerning taste and exceptional potential."

Ruhi's hesitation lingered, a testament to his independent spirit and refusal to be swayed by mere words. The voice, shrouded in mystery and allure, extended its hand gracefully, a silent invitation for him to submit to its guidance. But Ruhi, ever the rebel, scoffed at the notion of surrendering his autonomy.

With a swift and decisive movement, Ruhi evaded the voice's outstretched hand, a defiant act that sent tremors of uncertainty through the ethereal space surrounding them. As he broke free, a surge of adrenaline coursed through his veins, fueling his determination to escape this enigmatic encounter.

However, in his haste to elude the voice's grasp, Ruhi's calculated escape plan faltered. The ground beneath his feet became treacherous, betraying him at the worst possible moment. Like a fallen star, he tumbled into the depths of an unfathomable abyss, his descent marked by a torrent of swirling shadows.

CHAPTER FOUR

Eternal South

As regained Ruhi onsciousness, he found himself in a mysterious, dimly lit place. The air was heavy with an eerie stillness, and shadows danced playfully around him. .

In the depths of the mysterious dark place, Ruhi's senses heightened as he heard a hissed sound that seemed to call out his name.

In the depths of Ruhi 's disorientation, a voice emerged from the silence, its cadence laced with both familiarity and intrigue.

"Find a shelter soon," it urged, its words carrying an urgency that reverberated through Ruhi's very soul.

Startled, Ruhi's eyes darted around the enigmatic landscape, searching for the source of the voice. Yet, no figure materialized, leaving him suspended in a state of perplexity. Who could possibly be speaking to him in this desolate realm?

His brow furrowed with skepticism and a tinge of fear, Ruhi mustered the courage to question the voice.

"Who are you?" he inquired, his voice echoing through the ether, a blend of curiosity and caution.

A momentary pause followed, as if the very fabric of the universe held its breath in anticipation of the response.

Then, the voice resounded once more, radiating a gentle reassurance that seemed to transcend the boundaries of space and time.

"My name is Avignya ,I am your friend," it proclaimed, its timbre infused with a warmth that caressed Ruhi's uncertainty.

"I don't have any friends," Ruhi retorted, his voice laced with a hint of defiance. "And I have never seen you." His words hung in the air, laced with a mix of skepticism and yearning for understanding.

As Ruhi's words lingered in the air, a resounding laughter erupted from the depths of the mysterious realm, reverberating through his very being. The voice's chuckles danced like mischievous spirits, filling the void with an infectious energy.

"I am always present with you, my dear Ruhi," the voice replied, its tone carrying a playful melody. "But you have never turned back to see me. How can you claim to know me?"

Ruhi's eyes widened in astonishment, his mind struggling to comprehend the enigmatic presence that seemed to have been by his side all along. How had he been so blind? How had he overlooked the very essence that had accompanied him on his journey through life?

Before he could even entertain the idea of turning to face the voice, it interjected with a sense of gentle urgency. "Hold, dear Ruhi," it implored, its words a delicate whisper. "The time for knowing will come, but for now, focus on finding shelter."

As Ruhi stood there, captivated by the enigmatic voice that had accompanied him thus far, he felt a yearning to engage in further conversation.

But to his dismay, silence enveloped the surroundings, and the voice remained elusive, as if it had retreated into the shadows of the unknown.

Undeterred, Ruhi ventured forward, his determination fueling his steps. The mysterious place beckoned him with its secrets, its hidden corridors and concealed truths. He knew he had to explore, to unravel the enigma that surrounded him.

Suddenly, a rustling sound pierced the silence, causing Ruhi to freeze in his tracks. A hushed whisper, carried by the wind, reached his ears.

It called his name, its tone laced with an unsettling mixture of familiarity and intrigue. It was a voice he had not heard before, yet it resonated within him, stirring ancient memories and primal instincts.

Turning towards the source of the sound, Ruhi's gaze fell upon a towering tree. Its gnarled branches stretched towards the heavens, as if reaching for something beyond human comprehension. The tree exuded an aura of mystique, its presence both awe-inspiring and unnerving.

You called my name," Ruhi spoke, his voice betraying a mix of curiosity and trepidation. "Who are you?"

The tree's branches swayed gently, as if contemplating Ruhi's query. Then, a voice, ethereal and haunting, whispered through the air.

"I am but a guardian of this realm," it answered, its words carrying a weight that sent shivers down Ruhi's spine. "I have seen the ebb and flow of time, and I am privy to the secrets that lie hidden within the fabric of existence."

In a voice that resonated with ancient wisdom, the tree whispered, "Ruhi, within my hollows, find solace and respite from the mysteries that surround you. Come, seek shelter and protection within my ancient embrace..

As the invitation lingered in the air, Ruhi's gaze traced the tree's grandeur. It promised safety, an oasis of calm amidst the unknown. Yet, a flicker of something deeper stirred within him—a longing for exploration, for the exhilaration of uncharted paths.

He hesitated, his heart torn between the allure of security and the yearning for growth. The tree offered sanctuary, but at the cost of confinement—a life bound to a single place, void of the adventures that beckoned him.

You, a mere tree, dare to offer me shelter? I am destined for greatness, to conquer the realms that lie before me. I will not be confined to your hollows.

Your offer holds no appeal to one as magnificent as I am, said kshayank.With a dismissive wave of his hand, Ruhi turned away from the tree and continued his exploration of the mysterious dark place.

As Ruhi's tireless journey drew near its end, he ventured to the southern reaches of the vast cosmos. It was there, in the quiet corner of existence, that he stumbled upon a sight that stole his breath away—a magnificent palace, nestled amidst enchanting gardens.

The palace stood tall and regal, its walls adorned with intricate carvings that told stories of forgotten civilizations. Its architecture boasted a harmonious blend of elegance and strength, with towers that pierced the heavens and domes that reached for the stars. It was a testament to the artistry of the cosmos itself.

Entranced by its beauty, Ruhi aproached the palace with cautious reverence. As he stepped onto its grounds, he found himself enveloped in a symphony of colors and scents.

Exquisite flowers danced in the gentle breeze, their petals glistening with dewdrops. The air was perfumed with the fragrance of jasmine and roses, a sweet melody that serenaded his senses.

In the heart of the palace, he beheld a grand building that beckoned him with its allure. Its magnificence was elevated by the fluttering of colorful flags that adorned its facade, like vibrant brushstrokes on a canvas of dreams.

Vines of vibrant green wound their way around the structure, as if nature herself had claimed it as her own canvas. The foliage cascaded down its walls, breathing life into every nook and cranny.

CHAPTER FIVE

Transient Vessel

As Ruhi stepped into the opulent palace, his eyes widened with awe and trepidation. The grandeur of the surroundings enveloped him, casting a spell that seemed to transport him to a realm of ethereal beauty.

Sparkling lakes stretched out before him, their crystal-clear waters reflecting the sunlight like a million dancing diamonds.

Birds of vibrant plumage flitted through the air, their joyful chirping filling the atmosphere with a symphony of life. Majestic trees stood tall and proud, their branches swaying in rhythm with an invisible breeze.

Yet, amidst this picturesque scene, Ruhi's heart raced with a mixture of fear and fascination. For among the verdant landscape, he caught sight of fearsome creatures, lions and tigers prowling with an elegance that belied their raw power.

His instincts screamed at him to retreat, to seek safety in the face of such formidable predators. But a strange aura emanated from them, a calm and serenity that seemed to defy logic.

Summoning his courage, Ruhi approached the regal beasts cautiously, his eyes locking with those of a magnificent lion. To his surprise, instead of bared fangs and hostile growls, he was greeted with eyes that held wisdom and kindness.

The animals, as if sensing his presence, seemed to radiate an aura of tranquility, as though they were the embodiment of peace itself.

In awe, Ruhi reached out tentatively, his hand trembling ever so slightly. To his astonishment, the lion nuzzled against his palm, its rough tongue grazing his skin in a gentle caress. A sense of connection coursed through Ruhi's veins, an understanding that surpassed language and logic.

The animals, it seemed, were like enlightened sages, guardians of this idyllic sanctuary, entrusted with the sacred duty of embodying and propagating peace.

And so, in the company of lions and tigers, birds and trees, Ruhi discovered the true meaning of peace. In their presence, he learned that even amidst the wildest storms, the calm within one's heart could transform the world into an oasis of love and seren.

Do not be fooled by their allure, Ruhi," Avignya warned, his words carrying a note of caution. "Though they may appear loving and gentle, the path that unfolds in their company may not lead to a favorable outcome."

Ruhi's brow furrowed as he contemplated Avignya's words. He watched the animals as they moved gracefully, their peaceful presence captivating his senses.

Ruhi's heart raced as he approached the grand entrance of the beautiful building. The anticipation swelled within him, for he sensed that within those hallowed walls lay the answers he sought. But as he prepared to step forward, his gaze was arrested by a sight that sent chills cascading down his spine.

Emerging from the depths of the magnificent structure was a woman of unparalleled beauty. Her presence commanded attention, radiating an ethereal allure that left Ruhi spellbound.

Her eyes gleamed with ancient knowledge, while an enigmatic smile danced upon her lips. And beside her, coiling gracefully, slithered a serpent with not one, but five ominous heads.

The realization struck Ruhi with an electrifying jolt. This woman, veiled in elegance, possessed a power that transcended mortal comprehension. The snake, a symbol of both wisdom and danger, bore witness to her formidable nature.

But it was not only their presence that unnerved him; there, standing alongside the mysterious duo, were eleven soldiers, their eyes ablaze with unwavering loyalty.

Ruhi's mind raced, his instincts screaming for caution. He had ventured into a realm where power and intrigue reigned supreme. He knew that this encounter would irrevocably shape his fate, weaving him into a web of dark secrets and hidden agendas.

As the woman locked eyes with Ruhi, her gaze pierced his very soul. There was an unspoken understanding between them, an unspoken promise of untold possibilities.

Welcome, Ruhi," Jeevika's voice carried a tantalizing allure as she spoke his name, her eyes glistening with mystery. "My name is Jeevika, and I am a creature of this enchanting palace."

Ruhi's brows furrowed, a mix of surprise and curiosity playing across his face. How could this woman, who claimed to know him, have knowledge of his name when he himself was still lost in the labyrinth of his own identity? Jeevika's gaze intensified, her eyes seeming to hold the weight of ages.

She took a step closer to Ruhi, her voice dropping to a whisper. "Ruhi, my dear, the mysteries that shroud us are entangled in a tapestry of destiny and forgotten memories. We are bound by a connection deeper than you can fathom."

Ruhi's gaze met hers, a mixture of curiosity and skepticism evident in his eyes. "And who are you truly, Jeevika? How is it that you have come to reside in this magnificent abode?"

A wistful smile played upon Jeevika's lips as she revealed the depths of her enigmatic existence. "I, too, am plagued by the shadows of uncertainty.

My origins remain shrouded in the veils of the unknown, my parents forever a mystery. Since the moment of my birth, this palace has been my sanctuary, my only solace in this vast world."

Ruhi's eyes widened, his interest piqued by Jeevika's story. Her ethereal beauty and the air of mystique that surrounded her seemed to beckon him closer.

My, my, Ruhi," Jeevika purred, her eyes sparkling . "You certainly have an eye for beauty. I must say, I quite fancy you as well. Why don't you come inside with me? We can revel in the most exquisite pleasures this place has to offer for a glorious century."

"But darling, before we embark on this thrilling adventure," Jeevika whispered in a seductive tone", there's a little twist you should know. This magnificent building harbors not one, but several doors. Each door leads to a different kingdom, and you can only enter with a trusted companion by your side."

Ruhi's eyes widened with intrigue as he absorbed Jeevika's words, his heart pounding with excitement. The prospect of exploring multiple realms and uncovering their secrets enticed him further into Jeevika's enchanting web.

A playful smile curved Jeevika's lips as she continued. "Now, my dear, you must choose your companions wisely. They will be your guide, your confidants, and your allies in this grand journey.

Together, you'll unlock the doors and venture into realms beyond imagination. But remember, once you step through a door, you're in a different kingdom, and your destiny awaits there."

The building's secrets lay behind nine elusive doors, each with its own unique requirements. The first two doors are bound by the presence of a loyal companion named Mithra, their trust unlocking their mysteries. The following two doors find solace in the company of Pavan, for only with his aid can they be opened.

As we venture to the fifth door, a choice beckons, between the enigmatic Rasagnyudu and the elusive Vipanudu, both capable of guiding us through this threshold. On the right side, a door awaits, its entrance guarded by a faithful friend named Shruthidharudu.

Below the building, hidden from sight, lies another door, concealing its secrets in the depths. To gain entry, one must be accompanied by a steadfast companion known as Dhurmadhudu.

Behind the building, an arduous door awaits, reluctant to grant passage, yet yielding to the persistence of Lubdhakudu.

Lastly, there exists a door shrouded in fear, one that instills trepidation in all who approach. Known as Brahmarandhra, it stands alone, devoid of the need for any companion's aid, forever guarding its secrets. In reverence, we refrain from opening it under any circumstance, for its mysteries are not meant to be unveiled.

.And what better way to start this extraordinary journey than as husband and wife?" Jeevika's voice danced with a hint of mischief. "Ruhi, my love, let us seal this pact of exploration and passion.

Together, we shall conquer these realms, uncover their mysteries, and intertwine our destinies amidst a tapestry of enchantment."

Ruhi's heart raced, surrendering to the intoxicating allure of her charm. In a moment of blissful surrender, he embraced Jeevika as his wife, knowing that their union would ignite the flames of passion and guide them through the labyrinth of doors and kingdoms.

And so, Ruhi and Jeevika, bound by a love forged in desire and a shared thirst for adventure, embarked on a journey that would transcend time and reality.

They stepped through the doors, their destiny intertwined with the promise of kingdoms waiting to be discovered, and the echoes of their passion resonating throughout the realms they would conquer together.

Their lives are bound together in the most extraordinary way. Wherever she go, whatever she do, he will follow suit. If she eat, he will taste the flavors upon his own lips. If she sleep, he will feel the embrace of slumber in his own weary bones. And should tears grace hercheeks, his own eyes will glisten with empathy."

CHAPTER SIX

The Veil Of Destiny

"And so," Jeevika's voice echoed through the pages, her tone filled with an irresistible mystique. "As the final chapter of Part 1 draws to a close, dear readers, we bid you a temporary farewell. The intricacies of Ruhi and Jeevika's entwined journey, the answers you seek, lie beyond these pages, waiting to be unveiled in Part 2."

"Rest assured," Jeevika's voice continued, her words a velvet whisper. "The tale of Ruhi and Jeevika shall resume, weaving its spellbinding web anew.

The revelations, the trials, and the triumphs that lie ahead will leave you yearning for more, as their journey unfolds across the pages of Part 2."

So, dear readers, embrace the pause, indulge in the anticipation, for the answers you seek shall be revealed in due time. Until we meet again in Part 2, where destiny awaits with bated breath, and the enigmatic tale of Ruhi and Jeevika continues to unfurl.

CHAPTER SEVEN

As you reach the final pages of this captivating tale, I find myself compelled to invite you to embark on a voyage of imagination. I invite you to ponder the mysteries yet to be unveiled in the anticipated Part 2 of this saga.

I extend a humble request to you, dear readers, to share your visions, your speculations, and your wildest dreams for the continuation of this story. Your insights hold immense value, as they shape the tapestry of the narrative that will unfold in Part 2. I eagerly await your musings, your ideas, and your interpretations.

Kindly send your imaginings, your theories, or even your wishes via email to {SatishKoyidala@gmail.com} . I will carefully consider each submission, and the most exceptional among them will be featured in the next installment of this enthralling journey.

Your contribution will become an integral part of the story, intertwining with the author's vision to create a truly immersive experience.

Thank you for joining me on this enchanting adventure, and I eagerly await your correspondence.

Yours in the realms of possibility,

Koyidala Satish.

Printed by Libri Plureos GmbH in Hamburg, Germany